Live. Love. Learn.

A walk through infidelity,
love and acceptance

by

Tee Marie

ISBN: 978-0-578-45303-3
Editors: P31 Publishing, LLC
For more information, please visit www.authorteemarie.com

IG @t24marie
Facebook Tee Marie
Website www.authorteemarie.com
If you are interested in joining a Private Facebook Support Group please email info@authorteemarie.com

Back Cover Photo by Lisey Delgado
All artwork was designed by P31 Publishing Design Team
Any people depicted in stock imagery are models, and such images are being used for illustrative purposes only.

Printed in the United States of America

Dedication

This book is dedicated to my grandmother Doris Thomas a.k.a. Mother Dear for being a strong matriarch in my family, my late grandmother, Dolores Copeland, whom I never had the privilege to meet, as well as my great grandmother Christine Primus who gave me a lot of advice before she passed away, and last but not least, my two aunts Dyan Cortez and Dorothy Thomas, a.k.a. Auntie Dottie, who I miss deeply everyday.

Acknowledgements

I would like to take the time out to thank my amazing husband for just rolling over when I kept the lights on in bed writing away. He cannot stand any light while he is sleeping! I also, have to give my girls Tai and A.J. mad props for reading my manuscript at page 20, then 30, then 50 and motivating me to keep going. You two still haven't read it in its entirety, but I will be sure to give you two the first autographed copies! My friends Elizabeth, Tonya and Ebony J. and Ebony D., are more like family, who helped push me along the way and kept me motivated as well. I also want to thank my children for giving me time to myself periodically to write my book. When you're old enough, I hope you too will enjoy reading my book. Finally, I would like to give myself a pat on the back for being disciplined enough to complete my book that I was scared to finish in the beginning.

Last but not least none of this would have been possible without my amazing publisher and friend Jasmine Womack of P31 Publishing. Thank you so much for all of your guidance and support!

Thank you

I would like to thank all those who supported me throughout the entire process of writing my book. My sisters Nailah and Dawn, my parents Mark and Darcel Copeland, and I would also like to thank my amazing husband Everett Moss II for supporting me throughout the entire process, for pushing me to keep going and for being my back bone!

Table of Contents

Introduction

The main character in this book, Natasha, is a spunky wife and mother of five children. The couple experiences infidelity in their marriage and they have to decide if they will stay together. She and her husband seek therapy but hit a rough patch when a blast from the past comes to shake things up. They are faced with having to make a decision that can change their lives forever. Follow Natasha as she navigates her way through family life, relationships and motherhood. There are a few twists and turns that will catch you by surprise. So, buckle up and enjoy the ride!

Chapter 1

Allow me to Introduce Myself

Well I made it, I'm finally here. Where you might ask? I am finally at the place where I do not give a care. I do not care if someone does or does not like what I say or what I'm doing. I just simply do not care! It took me a long time to get here, over 30 years but that's it I am finally here. Who am I? I am Natasha Imani Smith, a black girl from a middle-class family who moved around a bit as a child. I come from a loving family of humble means, but we always had what we needed. I didn't always feel this way, in fact I used to be the type of person who cared a little too much about what others think or what their opinion about me was. I must admit that a small part of me still considers other's feelings, but I do not let it cloud my judgment. I was a daddy's girl growing up so wherever my dad went that is where you could find me. Although I was a tomboy I still made time for some girly things like Barbie dolls, hopscotch and occasional baby dolls, but my passion and when I had the most fun was when I was shooting hoops, playing tennis or football or watching any of the previously mentioned sports. No matter where we moved, my brother and I were always able to make friends, it came easy for us. We were likable people who enjoyed having fun and weren't afraid to do anything. Because of that, we tended to stay in trouble. We lived by the motto "snitches get stitches" so when it was time to rat someone out, we took the beating instead. We even came up with ways we thought were clever to ease the pain of the whooping. Like that one time when we decided that powder being put in our underwear was a good idea to leave a cloud of smoke for whichever parent was giving the beat down. We figured they would be choking from the dust while we make a clean getaway. It didn't work though, all we did was make them even more upset that we wasted their good powder on our foolishness! At the time though it seemed like a good idea. There were five of us in all but the two of us were by far the worst. Despite the trouble we found ourselves getting into, overall we were still good kids. All five of us knew not to bring home anything less than a C for a grade, so typically that was exactly the case. My interest in boys came a little early compared to the rest of my siblings. I remember in the fifth grade a little boy gave me money because he thought I was pretty and that was the first time I knew that someone was attracted to me. It was still too early for me to realize exactly what that meant. The next time I remember anyone paying any attention to me was probably the following summer. This boy gave me butterflies when anyone even said his name, Thomas. I had no idea if he felt the same way, but I later learned that he did. The problem with this crush was that first of all we were too young to even know what we were doing and secondly, we didn't even live in the same state. This was during the time of love notes and letter writing, the early 90's, so that's all we had to look forward to. He was a good guy but the timing and space between us just wasn't in our corner. There were more boys as the years went by but I was not "easy" so nothing lasted too long. That was until middle school when I met my first love, Antonio Harris. Unlike most first love stories, this was not love at first sight. In fact, initially I thought he was a clown and we were actually good friends. In addition to being a clown, he also had this bad boy side to him. He smoked weed and seemed to not have parents that were questioning him of his whereabouts. Eventually by him just being himself he won me over. In the beginning, we just enjoyed each other's company until physical attraction consumed us both. The summer entering eighth grade change my life forever. Yep, you guessed it, I lost my virginity. Although it happened early for me I can safely say that including my husband, I have only had four partners. How many thirty something-year-olds can say that? I am now a mother to five beautiful children of my own and they all have the same father. How's that for statistics! Not that there's anything wrong with anyone who does have more than one father for their children, after all if it wasn't for my miscarriages I too would have more than one father for my children. So, trust me when I say there is no judgment here. My children however do not know about my past but not because I don't want them to. They know what they need to know at the time that they need to know it. For example, my oldest girl was looking at a place where she had no business looking and stumbled across her older sibling's urn. She wanted to know why the name printed on this urn did not match our last name. Instead, the urn had the same last name as my parents. I carefully explained to her that when I gave birth to this child, who was no longer living, I too had that same last name. She inquired if he was my husband's child and I tenderly told her no. Her next concern was if I knew where that child's father was now. The answer to that question was also no. She seemed satisfied with my answers and that's where the conversation ended at the time. After all she was only around 9 or 10 years old at the time, so I felt that information was sufficient. That conversation taught me two things, one that my baby was growing up and two that I can handle anything that may come my way. I had escaped that conversation without having to answer how old I was when all of this occurred. When my husband and I were dating, we vowed to always be honest with our kids about our past and I had just gotten the opportunity to do so and it felt good.

Chapter 2

***

A Hard Life Begins

Over the years, I have struggled with finding my comfort zone. I am by no means an unattractive woman but I have allowed life circumstances to lower my self-esteem. Childbearing was the first life event to knock me down a few notches. Although I love my children with all my heart, with each birth I felt another piece of me slowly being chipped away. I do not know if there was anything my husband could've done to build me up but the fact of the matter is, I felt at an all-time low. You see, my husband is an extremely attractive, handsome, physically fit, self-driven, successful, get things done by any means necessary, go getting, likable, lovable, networking, make it happen kind of guy. He doesn't understand the concept low "self-esteem". He cannot grasp the thought of not being self-motivated. He views people like that as weak complainers who will continue to be where they are because of how they feel about themselves. The problem with that is, I am his wife. If I am feeling this way, is it not his husbandly duties to help lift me out of this funk that I am in? Surely this is not the person he fell in love with. How can we bring her back? I miss her too! Didn't he? You see, I wasn't anything to turn a nose up at either. In my heyday I was very athletic, knowledgeable about sports that most men watch but not many women were interested in. And overall, a pretty down chick. What do I look like? Well let's just say I was voted "most attractive" in my yearbook. Honestly, I was shocked to receive the recognition considering the majority of my senior year was spent off-campus, but nonetheless I won't argue with the facts. So here we are two desirable, attractive people starting a family with no clue what we were really in store for. We both thought that we were ready. Can you blame us though? Our legacies were our own parents who were still together after a few decades and are still together to this day. Our wedding was small because we didn't want too many guests. The limit was 100 guest and family pulled together to prepare the food. The night was absolutely perfect! Of course, my nerves were too bad to eat so as the reception ended I was famished! My husband obliged me and we went to the restaurant at the hotel for me to eat. Our wedding night was amazingly perfect. He was everything I needed and more! Although I can't speak for him I'll just say this, I PUT HIM TO B-E-D! The children came along two years later and they truly have been a blessing. Our son was born first and as most little boys, he is very attentive to me. I won't call him a mama's boy because he does have friends that he will leave me for in a hot second. He's always attentive to my changes whether it's my hair, nails or outfit he always notices. My girls on the other hand do not notice those things about me. It's funny to me how all 5 of my children are different in their own unique way. The girls each share dominant characteristics of either myself or my husband. The twins, Michelle and Kelly, seem to be in their own world most of the time. Shutting everyone else out. I like that though. It is like they are their own force not to be reckoned with. They stood up for each other at all cost and when one got in trouble the other wasn't too far behind. I will never forget the mystery of the missing shoes. The baby of the family, Yves, swears the twins destroyed her favorite teddy bear baby shoes. I keep all of my children's baby shoes and their first outfit that they wore home from the hospital in one room. My husband calls it a shrine and says that I really need to box the items up. But they were each such a blessing to me and are growing up so fast that I want to hang on to all of the memories I can. I caught Kelly and Michelle running out of my "shrine room" snickering.

"Hey, what were you doing in my room." I stop the girls in their tracks.

"Nothing", they both said in unison.

"Well it sure doesn't look like nothing", I reply.

Just then Yves comes running around the corner.

"What did you do with my shoes?!" cried Yves.

"Wait, what makes you think something happened to your shoes?" I asked.

"Because they said I was going to be two Teddy's short for not sharing my skittles with them earlier today."

I went and looked and sure enough her teddy bear shoes were gone. Neither of them ever confessed to what happened to the shoes but I bet they wish they would have. One month was the punishment for the crime, and they both had to put together their allowance to replace the missing shoes. My son Michael just shook his head at the girls' shenanigans. Our fourth child, Jessica, was very quiet. She only spoke when absolutely necessary and sometimes not even then. With a family as large as ours, one might forget someone at some point. Like the time we went to Macy's on Black Friday. There were so many people heading for the air fryer selling for $49.99 when it's usually $199.99.

As soon as the doors opened, I made a mad dash to the sale section and got the air fryer. The kids made a mad dash to the toy section and that's where I found them. Once everyone had what they were looking for, we checked out and were headed home. Everyone was so excited about what they found that we didn't notice that Jessica had gotten left at the store. Halfway home I quickly made an illegal U-turn and rushed back to get my baby. When we arrived back at the store, there she was in the toy section reading a book. Fortunately she didn't even know we left her. Thank goodness. Of course, as you can imagine, the other kids couldn't wait to tell her that we were almost home by the time we realized she wasn't with us and she was going to be spending the night because mommy forgot. It took me weeks and countless amounts of money reassuring her that I loved her very much and would never let anything like that happen again. Not to mention the reprimanding that I received from my husband. Needless to say, nothing like that ever happened again. I respect my husband I truly do but sometimes I do feel that he is too hard on me. We both work full-time jobs, but somehow all the responsibilities when it comes to the house and the kids are always ALL on me. Don't get me wrong, I know the Bible says that the woman is responsible for the duties of the home including the children and the husband is responsible for providing for the family. But if I am contributing financially too, can I get a little assistance in the house? This misunderstanding has been going on for years in our household. Me being the woman I am, for the most part, I have just gone with the flow. However, recently I have decided that I would do all that I can to keep the peace. Why am I trying so hard though?

CHAPTER 3

Disconnection

Somewhere along the line my husband decided to seek extramarital affairs unbeknownst to me. I mean this man showed no signs of being with other women. Well I guess if I was looking for something, I certainly would have been able to find it. I guess I was just so consumed with the household and the children that I just missed the memo. I must admit that ever since learning about his infidelity, I have had a sour taste in my mouth. Although, I eventually forgave him and we decided to move on, at times I catch myself staring at him in his sleep thinking of all the ways that I can get him back. Sometimes I see myself with my hands wrapped around his neck choking the life out of him. I should've suspected something when I saw him sweat every time I watched shows like

"Snapped" or "Fatal Attraction" that should've been my first clue. But for now, I will smile and bite my tongue. After all what will the children say? For the brief time that we were separated, according to them, this was all my fault. I left and took all four of them with me. All I heard for those few months were, "Mommy, why did you leave? Can we please go back? "What did daddy do? You left, he didn't want you to." There was something about hearing the man I would lay down my life for tell me that he has been intimate with 25 other women since we've been married starting from year number two of our marriage. A person can't help but think, what did I do wrong? What could I have done differently? Did I deserve to be treated this way? Did he ever love me? Was it the girl at the drive-thru who gazed into his eyes while she handed him back his card? Was it the hostess that seated us at the restaurant? These questions and countless others run through my head regularly. Yes, I mean even now. Everyone is a suspect. Is this normal? Do other men make their wife feel special enough after their indiscretions that they regain their self-esteem? It's been five years now and I still feel like any chick who wants my man can have a ride. Our sex life is good, the kids are cared for, the bills get paid and everyone eats, but yet I still feel like I'm not enough for him. Why? You ask. Well his social media following is excessive for a non-celebrity, plus he's not even a friendly guy. He walks around with a scowl on his face but obviously he will let his guard down if you're cute enough. Things were not always like this. I remember when we were dating, he worshiped the ground I walked on. He loved me so much that he ignored the fact that I had Herpes Simplex Virus 2 better known as HSV-2! (an incurable sexually transmitted disease commonly known as herpes). For the record, neither my husband nor children have been affected by the disease which leads me to believe I must have had a false positive reading upon diagnosis. Now do you understand why I thought he was the one? How many other men do you know who would enter a relationship that led to marriage knowing she has an incurable sexually transmitted disease? This too made me think that maybe my flaws are the reason that he stepped out on our marriage.

We had gone to a see a therapist in the past but because of the issues that we are having in our marriage, we decided to give it another try. As I sit here staring at the walls in this therapist's office, it just feels really cold. I'm not referring to the room's temperature, but the feeling I felt to my bones, was chilling. It was going to be a rainy day on top of everything else that was going on. I knew this because my C-section incision was a bit more achy than usual.

"So, How are you guys feeling today?" the therapist asked.

"All right." my husband answered in his extra deep voice.

"I'm OK." I responded in a meek voice.

"What brings you in today?"

"My wife doesn't trust me." Chase said.

"Tell her why!" I exclaimed as I rolled my eyes.

"She's holding on to the past and refuses to move on despite my efforts to assure her that she has nothing to worry about."

"Well what did you do in the past Mr. Smith to make her feel this way?"

"I had a few moments of weakness which resulted in me getting too close to other women. I apologized to her though over and over again. I try to reassure her that she is all I need and I've gotten the cheating out of my system, but no matter what I do she always brings it up. I know I was wrong but how long must I endure her judgment."

"Just so I can get a timeline established here, how long have you guys been married?"

"For 18 years." I reply.

"And how soon did the infidelity start?" she asked.

"Year two."

"And when did you find out about it?"

"Year 10."

"And how long has it been since his last indiscretion."

I gazed over at Chase and waited for him to reply this time.

"About 6 years now," he replied. I felt relieved that the number I had and the number he just said were the same.

The therapist was constantly writing every time we spoke. I started feeling sad and suddenly burst into tears. Not a sniffle, an all-out can't catch your breath, loud sobbing, snotting burst of emotion. She handed me tissue and told me that it was ok to let it out. Chase moved closer to me unsure if he should touch me or not. I looked at him as if to give him the OK.

The therapist asked me, "What are you feeling right now?"

I sobbed barely able to say the words.

"Why are you sad?" she inquired.

"Because our marriage is over and I'm so embarrassed to tell our children that I failed them as their mother. I was supposed to be able to protect them and keep them safe."

"Wow!", exclaimed Chase. "I thought we were here to repair this marriage not put a nail in the coffin."

I pulled myself together and sat up straight. "I cannot continue this way I thought I could but every time I close my eyes I picture you with another woman. If I close my eyes to pray, if I close my eyes to sleep, if I take a shower. If I am on top of you riding like a cowboy, I am always wondering did you spend the night with a woman? Did you shower with them the way we shower? Did they ride you better than me? Did they make your toes curl? Did they ask you to leave your family for them? Did you consider doing so?"

"ENOUGH!" screamed Chase. "Why are you so insecure? Ever since you gave birth you have not been happy with yourself. You are beautiful to me you always have been and you always will be. None of those other women matter. They do not and cannot compare to you. Please give me more time to show you that you are my one and only."

After a long pause of silence, I replied "I'm going to need a minute."

CHAPTER 4

Weighing Options

The next morning while on my morning run I thought about the first time my husband and I said "I love you." I thought about the look on our faces at the birth of each of our five children. I thought about the loss of our two unborn children. What was I thinking saying that I cannot stay in my marriage? Am I really going start all over again? I haven't been in the dating game in 18 years! I know I'm still cute but I have no game. And my kids would never go for me having a new man. They will give any man, other than their father, a hard time. I may have to beat them just for being disrespectful. At the same time I can't let just one run of clarity affect my decision. I must maintain my rationalism. As I re-entered the home Jessica, my 11-year-old, was waiting on me.

"Good morning Mommy," she said with her a little innocent voice

"Good morning my love. Did you sleep well?"

"Yes mommy, what's for breakfast?"

"I was thinking that I would make pancakes, bacon and eggs. Does that sound good."

"That sounds amazing!" Jessica said with extreme excitement in her voice.

"Good, now go wash up and brush your teeth. Let everyone else know that I am about to cook breakfast."

Just then Michael came downstairs and sat on one of the stools at the island in our kitchen. He looks so much like his father that it is actually scary. He's 18 now so he thinks it's OK to have adult conversations with me about my relationship with his father.

"So how are you holding up mom?" Michael asked.

"I'm ok son."

"No Ma, really, how are you? I noticed you and dad didn't really speak much once you got home last night. You had this really disappointed look on your face."

"Well son your father and I are definitely experiencing a rough patch right now but, I don't want you to worry about it though. I just have some things I need to think about."

"So why don't you just make a list of pros and cons? We did that in sociology class last year. You should try it. It will help you get a clear perspective."

"Listen to you schooling your mother on what to do about her marriage. I'll think about it son, but I meant what I said about you not worrying. Just make sure you're getting ready for college because the summer will go by fast."

Over the next few days I decided to take my son's advice. I made a list of pros and cons.

Pros

❑ He loves me.

❑ I love him.

❑ We have five beautiful kids.

❑ He's an excellent provider.

❑ We have fun together.

❑ He's loving.

- ❏ He's caring.

- ❏ He's attentive.

- ❏ I feel like he's my soulmate.

Cons

- ❏ He cheated.

- ❏ He's demanding.

- ❏ He's sneaky and deceitful.

- ❏ He is a liar at times.

- ❏ Flirtatious

- ❏ He broke my heart several times.

- ❏ Untrustworthy...

You know what? Maybe this wasn't such a good idea. I need a break. I decided to call one of my best friends to see if she could meet me for lunch. Fortunately, she was available. After an hour of girl talk therapy, I found myself in better spirits. This is a friend who had been married the same year that we were married and is now divorced. Unlike their relationship however, ours wasn't quite as ugly. Although my husband was unfaithful, he did always seem to have a certain level of respect for me. She on the other hand had to endure disrespect and mistreatment. I don't know which one was worse, having a husband who blatantly disrespects you and you're absolutely positive he's cheating or a husband who operates business as usual, no change to the routine, but behind your back he's really cheating. I do know that both circumstances are wrong but at least she saw it coming. My woman's intuition gave me just a slight tug on my heart. I tried to think of things to take my mind off of what was going on, so I logged into my social media account. Posting and sharing doesn't interest me much but at least I could see what was going on with everyone else. I, unlike most, only joined to keep in touch with family and friends separated by thousands of miles. It always put a smile on my face to see my cousins growing up, aunts, uncles and even grandparents. Yes, even my grandparents are all on social media. On this day in particular, I noticed I had a message on my account. I opened it and to my surprise it was from an old high school friend. We never attended the same high school but through mutual friends, we had somewhat of a relationship. The message was innocent. It read,

'Hey Tash! Long time no hear from. Looking good. Hope all is well. Blessings to you and your family. How are you?'

Was this a coincidence? Or was this a test? Could this really be innocent? Is this how my husband has been connecting with people all these years? Stop thinking. It's just an innocent message.

'What's up Q?! Good to hear from you. You're right, it's been a long time. I'm ok I guess, thanks for the well wishes. Take care.'

Was that too much I thought? Maybe I should've said that I was doing great. Oh well it's sent now. Oh I see he's typing a reply. Well here we go...

'Q? Wow no one has called me that in years! You really take me back girl. Good to hear you're ok, but why are you guessing about it? If I'm prying forgive me, but you don't sound ok.' (His full name is Carter but we all called him "Q". I'm not even sure why) So, do I reply with the truth or do I tell him I'm ok really? Just then my husband called me asking about dinner. My response was a curt "leftovers". Somehow, he thinks he's too good to eat leftovers. But based on the size of our family it is very rare we even have any leftovers at all.

"I'm not really interested in leftovers I'll ask our Chelley to whip me up something." Chase answered.

Chelley was his nickname for our twin Michelle. Of course, she'll jump to do anything for her daddy, which was cool with me. Besides her dream is to become a chef so any chance she got to whip up something extra she loved it! So that's what she did. Michelle got in the kitchen used random ingredients and made her father an amazing dinner. Meanwhile, I heated up the leftovers and finished up homework with Jessica and Yves, forgetting that I never responded to Q. I pulled out my cell phone and sent him a quick response, 'No, really I'm ok. It was nice hearing from you.' And I left it at that. After, we all ate, bathed and had a family game night, everyone was ready for bed. Nights like this reminded me that this marriage is bigger than just the two of us. The smiles, laughs and jokes that we all shared, always melts my heart. While doing our nightly ritual of brushing our teeth and discussing what we have to. Chase and I lay down for the evening. There were a few more necessary things to go over like bills and plans for the next day. After that business was handled, there was more "business" that needed to be handled. We have always been compatible in the bedroom and I will admit though that over the years the desire, for me, seemed to shift to a more emotional connection than physical, because of this I conscientiously make sure that we are intimate at least three times a week. Michael checked in with me on how my list was going.

I responded, "It's going."

He then said, "Well I just want you to be happy mom."

"I love you so much for constantly checking on my well-being. You will make an excellent husband to someone one day. I will be fine."

Since the housekeeper was scheduled to come today, I felt no pressure to stay home and make sure the house was tidy. With our youngest going to summer camp and all the older kids having plans with their friends for the summer, I went to the library to return some books and take a class at the gym. After class I hopped on social media to check in on my friends and family to kill some idle time. But of course there is a new message in my inbox. Immediately my stomach drops. I can't say it was butterflies but it was definitely something. 'I guess I did pry by asking about your uncertainty of being OK. If you need a listening ear or just a friend for distraction, I'm here. By the way I will be in town visiting family next month and I would love to see you. Maybe we can catch lunch. Let me know…Q'. So there you have it. I know what I should do but I don't know what I'm going to do though. I immediately pick up the phone and call my best friend,

"Felicia, girl you won't believe who wants to meet for lunch next month!", I exclaimed.

"Sure I can, it's either Jacob or Carter a.k.a. Q. Am I right?" Felicia asked in an 'I know I am right' tone of voice.

Jacob was an old friend of mine that I had several "situations" with. Our sexual chemistry was undeniable and there was no way anything innocent could come out of a meeting with the two of us.

"Oh man Jacob? Nah he and I could never go to an innocent lunch."

"What, and you and Q can? Not likely."

"Sure we can…" I replied. "You know Jacob and my chemistry is strictly physical. There was no need for conversation. Carter and I never crossed those lines so there should be no reason to do so now. Jacob was an on site situation." I giggled.

"You don't need to remind me. I was there!", replied Felicia "Ok so how did this come about? When is lunch? And why are you even considering going?"

"Well", I replied. "I received an invitation from him on Facebook and I haven't actually responded yet. I just called you first. I just have so much going on at home that it would just be good to have a distraction that will not make me think about my everyday life. I just think it will be cool to catch up. That's all."

"Will you be telling Mr. Chase about this meetup?" Felicia inquired.

"I don't think there should be a problem, I mean I'm always open and honest with him about everything, so he won't care. Bye Felicia."

"Keep me posted girl."

That's harsh. Should I even go to lunch? I mean it would be interesting to catch up, but is it really necessary? Surely since he doesn't live in the same state this will be an innocent lunch. I'm thinking too hard about this.

'Hey Q.' I start to reply. 'No the question wasn't too much. I have just been busy with everyday life. I actually don't keep up with this account much, but lunch should be fine. Just let me know the date so I can pencil you in. LOL! My number is the same. See you soon.' I logged off and really didn't think much more about it. I decided to go ahead and pick everyone up from camp early and get them ice cream. Our evening routine pretty much went the same as usual. Eat, talk, play, then time for the kids to go to bed. I decided to try to get a conversation with Chase before we both fell asleep.

"So how was your day?" I asked.

"It was decent, no complaints here. I got everything I needed done so I guess I can call that a good day. How was yours?" asked Chase.

"Quiet, I too had a pretty good day, no complaints from me either. Hey do you remember my friend from school? You met him not too long after we got married. Carter".

"That skinny dude with the big head? Yeah. Why?"

"He reached out to me and said he'll be in town soon. Would you mind if we meet up and had lunch? You're welcome to join."

"No, I'm not interested."

"So it's ok with you if I go?"

"Sure."

That night ended well, any night that ended with intimacy was always a good night to me. The next month went by fast. We managed to get by with minimal bumps in the road and one more therapy session. It seemed as though the happier I made myself, the more smooth our home life became. Chase seemed pleased, so for the moment life is good. It was the morning of my luncheon with Q and I just could not figure out what to wear. I figured I could call Felicia for advice, but she just made it worse. My final choice was a salmon colored sundress, short but not too short with some cute tan wedges and accessories to match. Although I gained weight, my body was always flattering in a cute sundress. And I know I'm not the only one to go commando in the summertime, so panty lines would not be a concern today. He chose the restaurant, a chic little hole in the wall named La Petite Maison, French for The Little House. The decor was very Parisian, with flowers and exposed brick walls. The menu was very light with the portions just enough so that you won't have any leftovers. Q was already there when I arrived. He rose at my presence and embraced me with a hug and a friendly soft kiss on each cheek, like they do in Paris.

"Ou lala!", he exclaimed as he took a step back and looked at me.

"Stop it", I said bashfully, as I tucked my hair behind my ear and looked down at myself. He pulled out my chair and pushed it in once I was seated. We sat there and talked for hours, until I realize it was time to pick up the children. I learned that he had never been married before, he had no children, and he was a top lawyer at a law firm in Boston. I wondered why he had never settled down and his simple reply was that he was too busy building his career and he felt that starting a family would only make him not be as successful at one of his tasks. And he wasn't willing to sacrifice his goals in his career that would in turn neglect his family of what they would need from him. I don't know if I think it's a load of crap or if I find it noble of him to make that decision. Either way all I can do is respect it. I must say it was good catching up.

CHAPTER 5

—◦◦—

Who is Karen King?

Months have gone by since our luncheon, and life for me was going well. At home, the kids were back in school, Michael was off to college and Chase and I were continuing our counseling and having date nights. For months our communication was getting better and everything seemed to be going smoothly, until I got a phone call from an unknown number that I typically send to voicemail but for some reason I picked up the phone.

"Hello?" I answer cautiously.

"Hello, is this Tasha?", a quiet sheepish voice asked. "Tasha Smith?" the voice inquired further.

I reply, "Yes, this is Tasha Smith. With whom am I speaking please?"

"This is Karen, Karen King. I don't know how to say this but, are you sitting down?"

"No, but you are starting to concern me. Who are you, and how can I help you?" I cautiously demanded.

"Well my name is.."

I cut her off, "You gave me your name already now what do you want?!"

"I have been trying to reach Chase about a situation from years ago. His number is not the same or I am blocked, but I was able to get your information. I really need to speak to both of you,"

"Are you an old friend? Or are you on some messy bull right now? I mean what's up?"

"I just need both of you please, no disrespect. Yes, I am an old friend of his."

"Well, I'm sure you were blocked or left behind for a reason. So, I'll call my husband for you hold on." I clicked over to dial his number. Palms sweating, heart racing, mouth feeling dryer by the second. The phone begins to ring and Chase answers at the second ring.

"Hey babe, what's going on?"

"Chase I need to ask you something and I need to stress how important it is for you to be honest with me right now."

"You got it babe, we're in a good space right now and I would like to stay there."

"Who is Karen King?" Silence. I could hear Chase swallow hard after my question. His voice cracked at his first words to me.

"She was one of the women I used to deal with when I was wilding, but I have not spoken to her in years, I swear." Chase assured me.

"Ok, well I have her on the other line, but before I merge these calls, is there anything else I need to know about her?"

"She was in the past and I would like to keep her there. Baby you are my future and that's it."

"Hold on." The phone clicks. "Karen?" I asked to see if she's still there.

"I'm here." She replies.

"Chase?" I ask confirming we're all here.

"I'm here too." Chase responds.

"All right Miss King, you have our attention."

As Karen spoke, I already knew what she was about to say. Call it women's intuition, call it a hunch, call it karma if that suits you. But I already knew what bomb she was about to drop. She explained that 8 years ago, when she was sleeping with my husband and several other women's men, she became pregnant. I mean this female was a home wrecking hussie on the loose! Here she is with this bastard of a child, out here looking for someone to be his daddy and she decides it's my husband's turn to take a DNA test. Now, although I am experiencing several emotions at this time, I think he should indeed take the test. See one thing my man has never been is a deadbeat dad, unlike some other trifling men I know. So we agreed to get the test done at the any lab test center of KK's choice (Yes I gave her a nickname). The day of testing I decided not to join Chase at the lab. After all, this test only had something to do with me if the results are positive. Other than that it was none of my concern. To my knowledge, she nor the alleged child had to be present for the test. The samples only had to be done at the same lab, but not at the same time. It will be exactly one week from the day he went that the results will come back. That week I must admit, I was no good! I found it extremely hard to focus on anything. I did use the time to reflect on all of the good my husband had done over the almost 21 years of marriage. I did this because if I chose to think of all of the hurt he caused, I may end up killing him in his sleep or better yet, slowly poisoning him over time. Instead, I tried to reflect on all of the loving times we shared over the almost 2 decades we have been together. Meanwhile, Chase has been walking around on eggshells all week. I noticed more drinking and less talking. Don't forget I have my children to save face for as well. It was important to me not to allow their routines to suffer from this new development that may end up being nothing more than a desperate cry for relevance from one of my husbands mistresses. The day of the test results I woke up optimistically prepared to receive whatever news was coming next. I tried to go about my day normally, but I couldn't help but feel sick to my stomach. I checked the mailbox at a time that I knew there was no mail. Once the mail was delivered, Chase had come home early to collect the results. As he peeled back the seal on the envelope, he looked me in my eyes and said, "Baby no matter what these results are, please know that I love you and I will spend the rest of my life, every day of my life, showing you how sorry I am for my past." With that said, the DNA test results read 99.999% probability that Chase Smith is the father of Kase King. Can you believe this? That heifer even gave him a similar name as my husband! I immediately fell to the floor in disbelief. Before I hit the floor, Chase caught me and held me so tight I thought I was going to burst. Once I was finally able to stop crying hysterically, I asked Chase how he felt.

His response was, "I really don't know, but I'm concerned about how you are."

"You have much more to worry about than my feelings. You have Karen and Kase now." I responded.

"Don't do that Tasha. Please don't do that. I'm so sorry and I hate that we have to go through this. But you and this family are my number one priority and you will continue to be that to me no matter what. We're going to need to work through this like adults."

"I need some air, I'll be back." And I left.

CHAPTER 6

Where do we go from here?

I didn't call anyone. I just wanted to be alone. So, there I was in my car driving to nowhere. There were so many thoughts running through my head. *How would we be able to get past this? What will the kids say? What will they think about their dad? What will they think about me if I leave? What will they think about me if I stay? What will our family say?* I decided that I needed to go somewhere I could just be still. I saw a nice hotel coming up at the next exit so I decided to check in. The first thing I did when I got to my room was order a bottle of wine. While waiting for the wine to arrive, I ran a bubble bath. For the next two hours I soaked, drank and cried. After I got myself together a little, I began thinking about this poor innocent child with no father, he deserved to have a father figure in his life. Especially a father who is as good at it as Chase is. So whether I like it or not, life as I knew it was about to drastically change. I've never spent the night away from the house unexpectedly so I didn't feel like I should now. I told myself I would just lay here for a little while first and then call home, but I ended up dozing off. By the time, I woke up it was midnight and my head was pounding. I had several missed calls from Chase and the kids. I decided to call him back, after all I had already forgiven him for the indiscretions back then, and he truly did not know about the child.

"Hello?" Chase said when he answered the phone. "Where are you? Are you ok?"

"Yes, I'm fine. I fell asleep at the hotel where I am now."

"Hotel? How long do you plan on staying there? Listen babe, I know what's going on is really messed up right now but I worry about you when I don't hear from you. You have every right to be mad at me and you can continue to be, but you got to check in with me just so I can know your safe. I know I just asked you how long you're staying but you don't have to answer that. Take all the time you need. I'll adjust my schedule for the kids and tell them that you went on a little me time vacation that you've been needing. Just tell me the name of the hotel and I'll put it on my credit card for your stay. I'll call you back in the morning to check on you. If you don't feel like speaking, text 'I'm OK'. I love you and I will spend the rest of my life making this up to you if you let me. Goodnight."

I was speechless. I couldn't answer him because tears were flowing down my face the entire time he was speaking. It took me a few seconds to hang up the phone. When I did hang up I text him the hotel information. The words that Chase just spoke to me reminded me of the way that things used to be when we were dating. I would have a problem and he would have a solution. He was always making things better. I stayed away for an entire week. I didn't call my friends but I did talk to my children daily. They would ask me, 'When are you coming home Mommy? Daddy doesn't comb my hair right.' Then I would hear Chase in the background telling them to stop asking me when I'm coming back. Just let me enjoy my break. Of course since I left so suddenly, I hadn't brought any clothes with me which meant I had to go shopping. Since Chase was paying for the hotel stay, I splurged a little. The everyday clothes I needed I shopped for as normal. But I did buy myself a very nice purse. Chase did as he said he would and called me every morning to see how I was doing. After my one week hiatus, I called Chase and asked him to meet me at a beautiful park in the city. I chose this location because it's a public place where other people are always around. Also, because the scenery is so beautiful that it will be hard for me to strangle Chase if a rush of anger comes over me. He showed up looking as handsome as ever. He had a prep boy look going on today with his polo khakis and his boat shoes. He had a bouquet of two dozen pink roses. Pink roses symbolize gentleness, admiration, grace and sweetness to name a few. You know I came with my A game. I wore a classy white dress with a nice pair of heels to set off the look. I thanked him for the flowers and he took a seat next to me.

He spoke first, "You look well. How was your week?"

"Thanks, it was enlightening and I feel like it was exactly what I needed."

"Good! Thank you for inviting me to meet you. I want to let you know that I have not contacted Karen yet. I felt that it was important for me to speak with you first. Do you mind if I share with you my thoughts?"

"Not at all, go right ahead." I responded.

"Although this is a messed up situation, I do not feel that the child should suffer. I have not ever been the type of man to neglect his children and I would not like to do that with Kase either. I understand if you do not want to come with me when I meet with Karen to discuss the arrangements for Kase going forward, however based on her previous track record I want to make sure that he is being well taken care of. I want him to meet his siblings and I'm thinking about having Michael come home from school this weekend to meet him if the schedule works out. What are your thoughts so far?"

As I was sitting there trying to listen to Chase and what he had to say, all I could think about was how all of our lives were about to drastically change. 'Do I really want to put up with this foolishness? I do not deserve this, my children should know their brother but I don't know if I can bear this.' It even sounds like Chase may be thinking about taking this kid on full-time!

"Tash?!" My thoughts were interrupted by Chase. "Did you hear me? I want to know what you think about what I just said so far."

"Yeah I heard you." I said confused and bewildered. "I'm not really sure if I want to meet Karen in person, I mean is that really necessary right now? The way I'm feeling is that, I don't want to meet her yet. I assume I may have to one day, but just not right now. I would like to meet Kase though. I want to know if he looks like our kids. Have you seen a picture of him at least?"

"Oh yeah, Karen has sent me a picture. Do you want to see it?"

"Yeah." Looking at the picture I felt like I was taking a trip down memory lane and looking at our oldest Michael when he was eight years old.

"He looks familiar." I said.

"Yeah, I see Michael too. Once the kids meet him I think they'll agree."

I look at him with a look of uneasiness. I'm trying really hard not to let my true emotion show. Here I am not the one who stepped outside of her marriage and I am the one walking on eggshells trying to spare his feelings. Is this a glimpse of what the rest of our lives will look like? Me holding back my feelings and emotions in order to spare someone else's. I don't think I can conscientiously do that.

"Well first things first, you talk to Karen and I guess we'll go from there."

After our conversation it was back to reality with my daily routine with the kids. My intentions are not to bring up Chase's conversation with Karen. I'll just sit back and wait for him to inform me about what happens. In the meantime, I'll check in with my family on Facebook. I just may need a trip to see my grandmother. Maybe if I go check in with her, then I will be distracted from what's really going on. I have the children to think about so I'll start with visiting for just the weekend and see if my mom can help Chase with the kids. That weekend I picked up the phone to give my grandmother a call.

"Hey Mima! It's Natasha. How are you?"

"Oh hey baby, it's so good to hear your voice. I'm ok baby just taking it day by day." Responded Mima. "How's my grandbaby and those great grandbabies doing?"

"We're ok Mima, everyone is getting so big they make me miss having little ones."

"And Chase?" asked Mima.

"He's good." I tried to answer without her noticing a voice inflection.

"What was that tone change I noticed? You're not calling to tell me you're pregnant again are you?!" Mima exclaimed.

"Oh no! Not at all. You don't have to worry about getting any more great grands from me. I'll leave that to my other siblings." I chuckle. "The reason I'm calling is because I want to come see you. I'm asking for a weekend of your time, just me and you. Girls' spa time, hair salon, shopping, whatever you want to do. So, what do you say, can you make time for me?" I asked with optimism.

"You know I always love to see you sugar, but why now during the school year? Aren't you going to bring the kids?"

"Oh no, not this time. I promise to bring them sometime soon, just not this time."

"Sure baby you can come. I'll see you soon, kiss those babies and tell them I love them. Send Chase my love."

"Ok. I love you, see you soon."

Over the next few weeks I prepared the kids for my trip with Mima for the weekend. I figured maybe after this visit I will be able to deal with our situation better. So I made sure Chase and the kids all had their instructions and I left to go see Mima. Chase was at work so I took Uber to the airport. He said he would take me but I told him not to worry about it. At this point I don't know what's going on with Chase, Kase or Karen. I did make one request though. I asked for the kids not to be introduced to Kase without me being there. Because of this Chase chose not to let them know about him yet. As far as I know, for the past few weeks Chase has been getting to know his son. I figure I will meet him when my children meet him. For some strange reason, I believe it will give my kids a new sense of trust between us to know that we will be experiencing this together. I've convinced myself of this so that's what I'm going to go with. When I landed in DC, I experienced childhood nostalgia. I went back to the wharf, the river boat dinners and all the trips we took to the local museums that I took for granted when I was younger. Now I wish we lived in a more culturally diverse part of the US. I picked up my rental and headed to Mima's. Her home was just as I remembered, plastic covering her living room couch, cast-iron skillets in the kitchen, pictures of all the children and grandchildren great-grandchildren and even great great grandchildren all around. I was met with a huge hug and kiss.

"How are you sugar?!" asked Mima.

"I'm good, how are you sugar?" I replied.

"Well you know as good as I can be, based on the circumstances. But I don't want to talk about me, let's talk about you flying out here, leaving my babies and Chase at home. Don't think I couldn't hear in your voice that something is wrong. I always know if something is wrong with my babies. It's a skill God gave me. So are you ready to share with me the real purpose of this visit?" she asked with the sweetest most sincere and concerned voice.

She knew me sometimes better than I knew myself. Probably because she helped raise me tremendously. I came to stay with her for a couple years of high school while my parents had a rough patch in their marriage. I just couldn't stand the arguing. I begged them to let me stay with Mima, under the guise of wanting to help her since she recently had surgery and could use some help. I did miss my siblings while I was gone but I definitely feel like our bond was strengthened since it was just the two of us those two years in high school.

"Yes Mima. You know me well, something has come up with Chase. Something that I don't know if I can move past this time. I think it has just gone too far.."

"Come on now child," Mima interrupted. "Don't get me all nervous just tell me what's going on, my heart can't take the suspense."

"Chase has another child." I blurted out. "This woman just showed up out of the blue from his past and dropped this bomb on me. Yes I said dropped it on me! Apparently she was completely blocked out of Chase's life. So she reached out to look for me!" I said now sobbing at this point.

"Oh sugar I am so sorry! How are the kids taking the news?"

"Well they don't know yet."

"So how long ago was this? And are you sure it's his? You know how thirsty trolls are, they'll say anything to steal your man or just shake up your household."

"This was about a month or so ago that he took a DNA test. But he's the same age as our dear little Yves. The little boy's name is Kase and he looks exactly like Michael when he was a child. Mima I'm not gonna lie, I feel like I've been punched in the gut this hurts so bad. I mean I don't think it's the child's fault so I would never want to be mean to him or push him away. To my understanding he's an only child so it would be nice if he was able to see what it would be like to have siblings. I think about how fun it was to have a brother and sisters. I just don't know if I can trust Chase again. I mean I know that this happened years ago, but I just think about the fact that if he had never cheated, and especially not being careless about preventing a pregnancy, we wouldn't be in this predicament. Not to mention exposing me to possible STDs. I just don't know what to do. How could he be so insensitive?"

"Oh hush child. I'm sorry you're taking it so hard but Chase is a good man. I know he has to be just torn up behind all of this. He's been a good man to you and those kids for many years. Have you made a decision about what you want to do yet?"

"No Mima." I sniffed. "I am completely lost. I feel like I just don't know what to do. For the past couple of years things have been pretty good between us, but this has always been my biggest fear. That someone from the past will pop up with some devastating news, now my worst nightmares have come true. I know he's a good man and that he loves me, but I just see his flaws when I look at him now. I feel like I need time away what would you do?" I asked hopelessly.

"With a good man like that, I would suck it up. Especially since this is not a new affair. The kids are not getting any younger and soon they'll be gone. Being single at your age is not going to be easy. If you can work past this, then you too can get back to the love you felt before you had any children at all. Just imagine, after all these years and all that you endured, reaping the rewards of your labor unapologetically living life to the fullest with Chase by your side. Baby girl, he's quite a catch and if you leave him he won't be single for long. Would you be able to watch him with another woman during his non-cheating mode? Doing things just the way you always wanted. She wouldn't even have to put that work in. Would you be able to handle that?"

"Mima I've thought about all of that trust me, I have. But I feel like I'm in a box watching my life happen around me. I'm emotional at the sight of him and it makes me feel bad. I mean if I have forgiven him and agreed to move on and I sit and keep silently resenting him that's not right."

"I know it's hard baby, do you have any friends to occupy your time? When your thoughts get the best of you it's not good to walk around carrying all this resentment."

"You might look at me different if I tell you what I'm about to say but I kind of want to get even, you know have my own fling. Do you think that makes me a hoe?"

Mima burst out laughing almost choking herself.

"Mima are you ok? What's so funny? You do, don't you? I'm not a hoe! I've been faithful him and only him for 18 years..."

"Oh hush child," Mima interrupts. "No one would ever be able to call you a hoe. If anything, you haven't experienced enough. You're always giving your everything, even when the knucklehead you were involved with didn't deserve it. You run around catering to Chase so much I don't even think you know who you are or what makes you happy. Your kids too. Your identity got mixed up somewhere along the way and it's time for you to find it."

She was right. All these years I have been defined by my family. I am either known as Chase's wife or the children's mother. Who am I?

"I think I'm gonna go lay down Mima if that's ok with you."

"Sure sugar, get whatever rest you need. Do you need something before you lay down?"

"No, I'm all right. Thanks Mima."

That weekend with Mima was exactly what I needed. We did everything she wanted to do and a few things I wanted as well. From manis and pedis to massages and shopping, we even visited the African-American Museum. We had lunch there, and the food was five star.

CHAPTER 7

Something New

Once the weekend was over I had a clear mind as to what I was going to do. I would sit down with our children, call Michael home from college, and inform them of their new sibling. I had already spoken with Chase about the idea so all that was left was to implement it. The plane ride home seemed to last for hours even though it was only a two hour flight. I didn't Uber home because Chase insisted on picking me up this time. It was great seeing him despite what was going on. He got out like a gentleman, carried my bags and embraced me with a hug and a kiss on my cheek. I asked how things went while I was gone and his response was,"I'm just happy you're back." He had taken the day off so we headed to lunch to discuss the situation at hand. I really wasn't ready to have this conversation but I knew it had to be done.

Chase started. "I met Kase over the weekend and he seems to be a pretty good kid. Although I do not agree with a lot of things that Karen does, she seems to have kept her foolishness away from ruining his spirit. He was a little shy and took some time to warm up to me, but at the end of the playdate I feel like we started building a bond."

"So where did you take him?" I asked.

"I took him to the playground, the one that has the ice cream truck that comes by. I feel good about the relationship potential with my son. I have to apologize to you again for all of the pain and heartache that I have caused and I know this situation may continue to cause. I promise to make you feel as comfortable as I possibly can and prove my love and devotion to you everyday."

I held his face in my hands and gently kissed his lips. I can't lie and say that I wasn't feeling some type of way about him bonding with his new found son. But I sincerely believe that Kase should have the opportunity to experience the benefits of having a great father, so I will stick to my original feelings about it. We finished eating and headed home. I decided to take a shower and invited Chase to join me. The moment we shared at that time was deliciously orgasmic! For those 30 minutes I almost forgot about the life-changing situation that we were facing. At one point I even found myself competing with people I never met. My thoughts were something like, 'I bet she didn't do it like this. And I bet she didn't make you feel like that.' I mean I took full control and was extremely aggressive. It was as if I was proving a point to myself, yeah I still got it and you know you still want it! Afterwards he went straight to sleep. I began prepping dinner and got ready for the kids to come home. I must say the evening ended well and for the moment I was happy in a way that I hadn't been for years. Chase and I decided to inform the kids about their new little brother. We sat them down and Chase began speaking first.

"You all know that I love you very much and nothing in this world will ever change that. Daddy has something that he needs to talk to you about. Yves you were not even born when I was going through a rough time in my life and I was not treating Mommy the way that she deserves to be treated. Everyone else here I'm sure remembers a time when Mommy and Daddy were not living together."

"Yes", the twins reply. Michael has an annoyed look on his face as if to say, 'Just spit it out already'.

"Well", Chase continues. "During that time, I was involved with another woman and she became pregnant. I had no idea because I stopped dealing with her and came to my senses about how much I was hurting my family by us being separated. Not being able to wake up and see each one of your faces everyday was eating me up. I had not spoken with this other woman for all these years until recently. What I am trying to say is, you all have a little brother who is 8 years old and his name is Kase."

At this point I interject, "Your father and I have talked about this and we would like you all, to meet him for the first time. I have not met him yet because I wanted to do this with you guys.

Although your father made a mistake in the past, it is not Kase's fault that he has never known who his father was. Please, I ask that you join me in supporting your father while we figure out how to embrace your new brother."

It took a while for Yves to really wrap her mind around the idea of how she can have a brother that's her same age. But the others seem to understand exactly what that meant and expressed their disappointment in their father. Since we have always raised our children to have an open mind, they were ok with meeting their brother and not blaming him for their father's mistake. After hours of explaining the best way we could to an eight-year-old, I think she finally understood enough to go to bed for the evening. It seemed like the more I tried to explain, the more questions she had.

It went something like this, "So I have a twin too?"

"No, baby. I would have had to have him in my stomach for him to be your twin." I replied.

"Mommy how can two women be pregnant at the same time?"

"Well, a man would have to lay down with two different women at two different times." I tried to answer her without showing too much emotion so that she could feel comfortable but also know that this was not ok.

Since the twins were good with Yves, I allowed them to help her with dealing with the issue at hand. The girls were sensitive to their sister's feelings. I actually felt a little more relieved because I knew they had each other whether that was the best way to deal with it or not I really don't know, but hey this is a new situation for us all and I'm learning as I go. For the next few days I was sure to pay extra attention to Yves since she was the youngest and they were the same age. That way she may be able to handle actually meeting Kase.

Now the day has finally come and we all get to meet Kase. I didn't know what to do so I did go pick him up a skateboard as a welcome to the family gesture. Michael made a section of his room "eight-year-old boy friendly" for Kase in the event he comes over while Michael is away at school. Chase went to pick up his son without anyone else, because I am just not ready to put a face to the "homewrecker". Don't get it twisted, my vows and commitment were with Chase not KK. However I do not have respect for a woman that intentionally sleeps with a married man. She knew I existed and despite that fact, she still did not take precautions as a woman to ensure that she did not become pregnant. Chase on the other hand did know what could happen by him not doing what he was supposed to and that he could potentially lose his whole family behind this bad decision. Regardless of all of that, here we are and I am just not ready to meet her yet. Up to this point, I have not had a face, let alone a name to put to any of my husband's indiscretions. Kase was a very handsome young man and seemed to have been trained to use his manners in a room full of strangers. We tried to make it a fun loose environment. For his first visit, instead of greeting him as if it was a family meeting we did a barbecue. And you already know Michelle was my main help with all the preparations. I must admit at first it was awkward. Kase hung up under Chase and that made Yves a little jealous, but by the end of the night no one wanted Little Man to leave. Yes that's my nick-name for him already. I'm such a sucker. I've always wanted to have another little boy so he really is doing something to me that I can't quite explain. Michael was my only boy and nothing but girls followed. Once we all said our, 'see you next time goodbyes', Chase drove him back to Karen. She lived 30 minutes away so he wasn't gone long. That night was a success and everyone seemed to be ok with the situation. How could I move past my emotions and learn to accept this new addition to our family? Would I really be able to? I decided to confide in my friend that I know has gone through a divorce already. I typically exclude her from all the details of what's going on with me in order to protect her from reliving her own pain and turmoil. I cautiously led up to my reason for reaching out to her on this particular occasion. To my surprise she was open to providing me with her take on the situation.

"Tasha I'm not gonna lie," Aubrey began. "As difficult as it is for me sometimes to accept that my marriage failed, my peace of mind is so much more important to me. You see I held on to David for so long because of what it may have looked like to everyone else that knew us and supported our union. I had been extremely unhappy for quite some time, the truth is if I would have been ok with him having rendez-vous with other women and accepting that when he was with me, it was my time. We would still be together. But what way is that for me to treat myself? What example was I showing my daughter about how a man is supposed to treat a woman? After I forgave him for his indiscretions and forgave myself for playing his fool, I made the decision to part ways with the love of my life. Let me ask you something. Despite the fact that Chase has a child who is the same age as your youngest Yves, do you feel that he is still cheating on you now?"

That was the question of the century!

"There are times that I feel like his attention may be elsewhere. Like he may be too friendly with his "fans" but deep down, no. I do not feel like he's being intimate with anyone else right now. Although I do not appreciate the entertaining of other females, I have learned that as long as I know I am doing all that I can and am supposed to do, I will not have to feel guilty about anything anyone else does against me."

"Well since you don't think he's cheating, then you really just need to make a decision about how much you can handle and what you want to do. You have five beautiful children to think about plus your own comfort. Michael is grown so technically the girls are the only ones that will be coming with you, in the event that you leave. Have you spoken with someone professional about this." Aubrey asked.

"Probably not as much as I should have, but I guess I can still do that. You know I just want him to understand how I feel. I mean how I REALLY feel. He takes me for granted in a lot of ways. I really don't think that after all these years I should be feeling so insecure. I just want to know that someone cares about me enough to put me first. Is that too much to ask?!"

"No."

Aubrey gave me a simple one-word reply. Her response let me see just how reasonable my request was. I sure had a lot to think about.

CHAPTER 8

Dr. Hayes

decided to schedule a session with a therapist. She was a kind, down-to-earth woman I found on our insurance company's website. After we exchanged our normal salutations, we got right into my story. I talked and talked about how I love my husband and how much it hurt me that he stepped outside of our marriage. I also talked about how I wish I could forgive him to the extent of not thinking about his indiscretions so much, that sometimes those thoughts consumed my entire day. Dr. Hayes response however, was not one that I expected.

"Mrs. Smith," she started. "Have you ever considered having an affair of your own? Before you respond I would like to share a story with you. I have a group of friends that I went to college with and we called ourselves the "Fly Girls". This was not just the name that we called ourselves but anybody who was anybody called us by this name as well!" She said with a smile on her face as if she was reminiscing on a specific situation. "We would have so much fun that we would pride ourselves on not being in relationships. Although we were not excessively promiscuous, we had our fair share of 'experiences', if you know what I mean. Today all of us are married but still get together once a year to relive our heyday. We always take a trip not too close to home, in order to avoid seeing anyone who may recognize us. That also means that our annual trip has to be planned on an off season for travel. Meaning no holiday weekends! The chances that we run into anyone we know is very slim. Do you get what I'm trying to say? Do you have some girlfriends you can take a trip with?" She genuinely asked.

"Are you implying that I take a girls trip in order to have an affair of my own?" I stared at her wide eyed in disbelief for about 10 seconds before I could make a sound come out of my mouth. When I did finally make a sound it was a burst of laughter!

"You can't be serious right?! That was a good one!" As I open my eyes from wiping the tears from laughing so hard, I noticed her facial expression and she was not joking.

"That will be all for today Mrs. Smith. Think about what I said and let me know what you come up with at our next session." She stood up and extended her hand for me to shake.

Well I guess I truly offended her. I didn't mean to insult her with my laugh I just thought it was an absurd suggestion. Oh well, I still gave her a firm handshake and left. My drive home was quite interesting. I just could not stop thinking about the doctor's proposal. She was the licensed professional after all, maybe she knew what she was talking about. Don't get me wrong I don't see myself capable of being intimate with another man besides my husband, but the idea that I needed to get away on a girls trip could be exactly what I needed. So I made a few phone calls and within a couple of months the trip was planned to Cabo San Lucas, Mexico! By the time we were all ready to go, it was planned on a holiday weekend despite what the therapist said. Labor Day weekend to be exact. There aren't many women in my circle so the trip consisted of myself, Felicia, Aubrey, Lisa, Linda, and Savannah. Each of these women, at some stage of my life or another, have played a significant part. Thankfully, because I know how to choose my friends, we all get along well and were ready to enjoy our time away. As soon as we landed, we were met with drinks, a mariachi band, and to my surprise a blast from the past! I could not believe my eyes, there was Q across the resort lobby sitting at the bar looking as handsome as I remember. His eyes caught mine and we smiled at each other. What were the odds that I run into him here? I guess this was the reason that the therapist said NOT to travel on a holiday weekend. Felicia pinched me and I chugged down my margarita drink like I was at a college frat house party. 'Here goes nothing', I thought. Q got up from the bar and began walking in my direction, I wanted to look away. In my head I said, 'MOVE GIRL!' Move your head, an arm, your feet. Move something!' But I couldn't. I was stuck. My eyes locked into his body, mine slightly trembling and my heart was pounding so hard that I just knew everyone there could hear how loudly it was beating. I even felt like they could see it beating so hard it was about to rip my chest open!

"Hello beautiful." Q said in a smooth sexy tone.

Now my knees were turned in and touching each other and I could feel them getting weak. He placed his arms on my elbows as if to steady my balance. I adjusted my stance so that I was standing up right again.

I opened my mouth to say, "Hey buddy." What a dumb way to greet my childhood friend of so many years. He laughed and I giggled.

I could feel Aubrey's eyes glued to me as if she was waiting to see what I was going to do next. I glanced at Felicia and she had the straw from her drink at the tip of her lips as if she was watching a movie waiting to see what was gonna happen next. The rest of the girls were watching from the sidelines but also taking in all the scenery of this beautiful resort. I broke focus on Q, grabbed his hand and introduced him to those in my crew that he did not know. Of course he knew Felicia. She and I went as far back as high school. Everyone else I met after graduation. Once I realized I had been holding his hand the whole time, I dropped it like I had touched something hot on the stove. I put my hand over my mouth once I realize that everyone noticed how dramatic the release of his hand from mine was.

"So.... let's go ladies. I'll check in and see where we're going to be. See you later Q."

He opened his mouth to say something but I was sure to keep moving forward as if I didn't hear him. My girls followed suit. He has my number so I'm sure I'll hear from him again once we get settled in our villa you know. All eyes were back on me.

Savannah started, "Chick! Would you like to tell us what that was all about?!"

Let me tell you a little bit about Savannah, she's the friend that doesn't take crap off of anyone. I can't talk to her about anything in regards to Chase because her advice would be, 'Leave him! Take the kids and go!' So I must be cautious in how I answer her question.

"What do you mean?" I reply while pinching Felicia not to let anything out.

"Female dog, don't act like we all didn't see that. Come on, y'all saw that right?" Her voice got more high pitched as she solicited for company in her observation.

Lisa, Linda and Felicia all chimed in, but Aubrey just sat back with her, 'don't go there' look on her face.

I let out a big sigh and finally said, "Ok so, I told you his name. Well his real name is Carter but we have always called him 'Q'. He's a friend from high school and I haven't seen him in a long time. I thoroughly wasn't expecting to see him here."

"Yeah but you looked at him as if no one else was there and we were standing in a lobby full of people.

And need I remind you that you are married to an ex-cellent provider and have five beautiful children. Did I miss something? Is Chase screwing around again?"

"Honey I'm going to need another drink before I participate in this interrogation." I responded.

Just then Felicia comes out the kitchen with a drink right on cue. I take a gulp and answer the last question first, "No, Chase is not messing around. It's just good to see an old friend that's all."

"Mmmhmmm." she replied.

"So what's the move for tonight ladies?" asked Felicia.

Just then my phone alerts me that I have a new message. I looked down to open the message and Felicia notices me looking at my phone.

She clears her throat, "Can you please engage in this conversation?"

There she goes calling me out again. "I'm paying attention. I'm down for whatever. I just have to go to the bathroom first."

Felicia rolls her eyes because she knows exactly what I'm going to do. I give her the look and mouth through my teeth, 'you better not!' She nods and keeps urging the girls to come up with evening ideas. In the restroom, I pulled out my phone to check my message. As I expected, the message was from Q. In an ironic change of pace, I decided to exit that message, and send a message to Chase letting him know I arrived safely. He replied that he's glad to hear that I made it safe and wished me well. He also put me at ease about the kids being ok and let me know that he loves me and hopes I get everything I need from this trip. I sent a quick cute kissy face and moved on to the next message.

The message simply read, 'let's meet for drinks.'

I simply replied, 'ok'.

In my mind this was not such a bad idea. After all two friends can meet up for a drink, right? I flush the toilet to keep up the façade of using the restroom. I washed my hands and splashed some water on my face. As I looked at myself in the mirror I said, "You are going to do this and you are not going to explain yourself to anyone! You got this! Let's go!" I open the door and broke the news to the girls.

"Did you ladies decide what you wanted to do tonight?" I asked but could care less.

"We decided on dinner and sightseeing. We figure we will search out the land to see where the spots are that we want to hit up for the rest of the trip." replied Aubrey. You know she is the responsible one.

"Cool," I said. "That sounds... responsible. Well, I will not be joining you ladies this evening, however I decided that I'm getting drinks here on the resort with my friend Carter. Before any of you say anything, I don't need to hear anything about it being a bad idea, I have already decided I'm going no matter what any of you have to say."

To my surprise no one objected. They told me that they want me to be safe and encouraged me NOT to leave the resort. Actually, it was more of a threat. I agreed and we all began getting ready for our evening. The ladies left and I waited. Twenty minutes later my phone rang and we agreed to meet downstairs. As expected, he beat me to the lobby. We talked, we laughed, we reminisced, we just had an amazing time! We had so much fun that neither of us wanted it to end. We found another spot on the resort to listen to music and dance. It was like a hole in the wall club with extremely dim lighting, strong drinks, amazing salsa music and wall to wall dancing EVERYWHERE! And boy did we dance! I felt so comfortable and free on the dance floor. The drinks were flowing and the salsa music was playing. Dancing Salsa was a very sensual type of movement and everyone was feeling the buzz of our drinks. To our left and our right all I saw was hips swaying and bodies rolling. Before I knew it my dress was rising and I was letting it happen. Q was dancing behind me holding my waist gently leading this dance. His hands were gently running up my thighs and in between my legs. I raised my hand up and grabbed his neck laying my face against his. I could feel my body's excitement and again, I just allowed it to happen. This was it! I knew what was next. But was it really going to happen in the middle of the dance floor in Mexico with a man who was not my husband? The answer was yes. Yes it did! He was behind me holding me tight and I was as free as a bird. Although we had done something dirty and erotic he was a complete gentleman afterwards. He walked me to my villa and sealed the evening with a gentle kiss to my forehead. That was it. No conversation. No regrets. Just a beautiful end to an unexpected evening. I walked back into our villa feeling good and guilty at the same time. What had I just done? Am I now the same as Chase? How can I be upset with him for doing exactly what I just did? The girls weren't back from their night out yet. So I was eager to hop in the shower. I scrubbed and scrubbed and scrubbed until my skin felt sore! Is this how Chase felt in the beginning of his infidelity streak? And if so, how the hell could he keep going? There are so many thoughts and questions racing through my mind right now. Ok girl, just breathe, I thought. Just empty your mind and breathe. By the time I got out the shower, I could hear the girls coming back into the Villa. I tried to hurry up so that I could appear to be sleeping once they stumbled back to my room. I already know who will be the first one to bust through the door.

"All right Chick. SPILL IT!" Felicia demanded.

A more reasonable Aubrey followed close behind. "Now, now, Felicia. Give her a chance to let us all in on what happened. The rest of them are not too far behind."

"Lisa! Linda! Savannah!" Felicia hollered. "Get your butt in here if you want to know if Natasha is still our faithful friend!" I patiently waited while the other girls made their way to the room. I sat up and took a deep breath.

"We had a good time together," I said softly. "We went out and danced and I felt like I was in high school again. I mean the DJ knew just what songs to play. As a matter fact," I tried to change the subject subtly. "We should go to that spot tomorrow night. You guys would love it!"

"You ain't slick!" Felicia interrupted. "I know what you just did there. Don't think you can just woo us with your info about the joint and not tell us if you gave it up or not. Did you give it up or nah?"

"I'll just say this, we had a great time together."

Each of their expressions were almost identical. A blank stare where they managed to just blink once. I knew they didn't believe that my evening was innocent, but hey they let it go and so did I. I didn't see Carter again for the rest of the trip, because I asked him for space and that's what he gave me. It wasn't easy getting him to back off, but ultimately he respected my position. That this was a one-time mistake that wouldn't be happening again.

CHAPTER 9

Daydreaming

A lthough I never confessed to the group what had actually taken place, they knew I was returning home a changed woman. The entire plane ride home, however I couldn't help but think about what I was going to tell Dr. Hayes about the way that I misbehaved on this trip. After laughing so hard at her suggestion to do what I had just done. It made me sick to my stomach. How was I going to tell Chase what happened? I closed my eyes and began to pray. I prayed long and hard about forgiveness and understanding and for courage and clarity. I needed to forgive myself for breaking my marriage vows and I needed God to forgive me for disobeying his laws and his commands. After my prayer, I felt some sense of calmness come over me. I felt like I could get off this plane with a new sense of womanhood under my belt. One where I take responsibility for myself and my actions. One where I am unafraid of the consequences for my actions. One where I am woman enough to confess my wrongs. One where I am human enough to know that this information will most likely rip my husband in half. One where if my husband cannot continue on with me, I will have to accept my new life only having Chase as a friend. This woman will accept all responsibility and consequences for her actions. So here goes, the girls and I say goodbye and take off in our separate car services. On the ride home from the airport I decided to take out a sheet of paper and write,

"I am ok."

Chase greeted me as I entered the house and the kids weren't too far behind him. I handed out all of the souvenirs and told Chase that I needed to talk to him.

He replied, "Sure babe, what's up?"

I took him to the basement where we could have some privacy and shared with him what took place in Mexico. I apologized to him for breaking my vows and asked for his forgiveness. I let him know that I would be ok with whatever he decides to do. I also let him know that he can take his time making his decision.

I felt like we were young again and I was waiting for him to let me know if he would stay with me after learning I had a non-curable STD. He did give me the courtesy of thanking me for sharing the truth with him right away, but also let me know that he would have to think about his decision before giving me an answer as to what he wanted to do. A couple of weeks went by and we continued going on business as usual. We slept in the same bed and communicated throughout the day. That was it. Nothing more, nothing less. Two weeks after that he was finally ready to talk.

"Tash, you know I love you more than I love myself. The sacrifices you make for our family is unparalleled. The way that you accepted Kase as one of our own, was the sexiest thing I've ever seen you do. I know that my indiscretions have been more than a few and I am grateful for your forgiveness and acceptance. I'm not gonna lie though, hearing what you told me made me feel like someone walked up to me and punched me so hard, the wind got knocked out of me. Never in a million years would I have thought that you were capable of this. I mean, I know you're only human so mistakes will be made, but you remained faithful for so long that I just thought that you would forever be my "good girl." And I would be the only screw up."

I raised my eyebrows and felt my eyes widen, I felt tears coming but I refused to let them drop. Is this man really telling me that I am a screw up for one indiscretion in comparison to his uncountable offenses?! Is he really going to sit here and beat me down while I already feel horrible about my one mistake?! Let me just calm down and try to hear him out.

"Tasha! Tasha! Are you ok?" Chase asked.

"What do you mean? What's going on?"

"You were squirming and sweating. Frowning up and even kicking your feet a little bit. Like you're having an intense dream or even a nightmare. Are you ok love?"

Oh shoot! You mean to tell me I've been dreaming this whole time? So I'm not a cheater, I think to myself. And it makes me smile at the thought. I began laughing hysterically.

"Tash? Are you losing it?" Chase is now looking at me in disbelief as I crack up out of a dead sleep. I pull myself together so that I can answer him and put him at ease.

"I'm fine dear." I reply. "I just had a hilarious dream."

"Do you care to share?" Chase asked inquisitively.

"Umm, I don't think you will find it as funny as I did. Maybe some other time." I said and roll back over.

"Ok, if you say so."

He wrapped his arm around me and that was that. The next day I scheduled a session with Dr. Hayes. I just had to share with her my dream that was clearly initiated by her ridiculous recommendation that I actually cheat on my husband. This would also be my last session with her. Eventually, I would share with Chase the ridiculous suggestion made by the doctor.

Over the years, our relationship has been strengthened by our trials and tribulations. The children get along very well with Kase and I'm beginning to forgive their father for having another child outside of our marriage. I must admit, I love that little boy as if he is our own. Karen decided that it would be best for Kase to live with us full time so that he can be raised by his father and grow up with his siblings. We have full custody of him and things are going great! Kase visits his mother every weekend. Even

Karen has moved on with her life and is in a committed relationship with a man that respects our situation. Overall I would say we have a good life. Despite our ups and downs we have intense, extreme love for each other. Are we perfect? By no means, but we are both willing to continue putting in work. As long as two people are willing to WORK any obstacle can be overcome. If someone would have told me years ago that I would forgive Chase for having another child, I would have bet money that I WOULD NOT! The potential that we saw in each other from the beginning is still there. The secret that no one tells you when it comes to marriage is that you will always be working on it. There is no "safe zone" or "seven-year itch". You will every single day have to work on your marriage. And the truth is, what you put in, is exactly what you get out. Anything worth having, is worth fighting for. After all, you wouldn't come in to work expecting to put in zero effort and receive an Employee of the Month award or a life-changing raise would you? If you do, then you are unrealistic! The same goes for marriage, you cannot be rewarded for something you didn't work for.

Epilogue

There are many lessons to be learned in this book. The main character shows intense love for her husband and kids throughout the book. She has many relationships that she maintains. Wife to husband, mother to child, granddaughter to grandmother, and a few different friendships. The fact that she is able to maintain friendships from childhood as well as build new ones shows that she has integrity and is a loyal person. She also understands the importance of balance. Although she has friends with different personalities, their differences complement each other's strengths. Her best friend, Felicia, is the crazy friend who keeps the humor and fun in every situation. Aubrey is the friend that is reasonable and analyzes every situation so that a sound decision can be made. Carter reminds Natasha of a time when life was carefree and full of fun. Mima, Natasha's grandmother, helps her to see that she needs to weigh both the good and the bad before she makes a decision. Her oldest child,

Michael, let's her know that she doesn't have to act like she is ok if she is not. Taking a step back and evaluating all factors involved in decision making, can be a huge benefit. Her younger children help her to see that innocence is a luxury that adults no longer have once they begin to experience life. So, she needs to allow them to enjoy the most of life before more serious things become a priority. She also has the memories of her childhood spent with her own siblings. The mischief she and her brother got into as well as her sisters. Natasha also has to process the relationship that she witnessed growing up with her own parents. All of these life experiences mold her into the confident woman that she becomes toward the end of the book. She learns to love herself and accept that it is ok to take care of herself before she is fully capable to care for others. If you have ever flown on a plane you have heard the announcement made overhead about putting on your air mask first in the event of an emergency. The purpose of that announcement is to ensure that you do not pass out from lack of oxygen before you are able to help anyone else. The same is applied to life, if you are not ok then you will not be able to ensure that others are ok either.

Synopsis

nfidelity is never an easy thing to experience, but that is exactly what the main character, Natasha, encounters. The different phases that she goes through are all necessary to make it to the other side. Emotions from both she and her husband are valid and should be recognized.

Natasha finds herself in an uncomfortable situation when one of her husband's mistresses returns with some information that will change their lives forever! The decision to keep the family together or separate will be one of the hardest things that she has ever had to deal with. As a wife and caregiver for their children, she will have to weigh all options. The family will either be built up or torn down.

About the Author

Tee Marie was born in the South Bronx, New York and was raised in Northern Virginia. Her family finally planted themselves in Georgia, where she graduated from high school and currently resides with her family.

She has been married for 13 years and has 3 beautiful children.

(The experiences shared in this book are based on true life events. My hopes are to help other people who may share similar experiences or even the same exact experience, to know that they are not alone.

There is hope on the other side to find true happiness and peace within yourself. You do not have to become a victim of your circumstance. Self-care is the key to happiness. You are enough, and you are worth the fight.)